P9-DCP-581

SANTA COWS

SANTA COWS

By
Cooper Edens

Illustrated by
Daniel Lane

GREEN TIGER PRESS
Published by Simon & Schuster

New York London Toronto Sydney Tokyo Singapore

GREEN TIGER PRESS, Simon & Schuster Building, Rockefeller Center,
1230 Avenue of the Americas, New York, New York 10020
Text copyright © 1991 by Cooper Edens
Illustrations copyright © 1991 by Daniel Lane
All rights reserved including the right of reproduction
in whole or in part in any form.
GREEN TIGER PRESS is an imprint of Simon & Schuster.
Manufactured in the United States of America.

10 9 8 7 6 5 4 3

Library of Congress Cataloging-in-Publication Data
Edens, Cooper. Santa Cows/by Cooper Edens:
illustrated by Daniel Lane.   p.   cm.
Summary: On Christmas Eve a visit from the Santa Cows
brings gifts and the spirit of peace.
[1. Christmas—Fiction. 2. Cows—Fiction. 3. Stories in rhyme.]
I. Lane, Daniel, ill. II. Title. PZ8.3.E21295San 1991
[Fic]—dc20   91-57G
                                                                            CIP

ISBN: 0-671-74863-7

For Tom and Mary
D.L.

For Mr. & Mrs. Leo
C.E.

'Twas the night before Christmas, and in our duplex
The children were plugged into special effects,
While pizza with sausage and peppers they downed
With soda, plus popcorn and chips by the pound.

Then while all the children the TV were viewing,
The sound from the kitchen was purposeful chewing,
As Elwood with clamcakes and I with chopped eel
Had just settled down to our microwave meal.

When all of a sudden, not the sound of reindeers,
But the mooing of Santa Cows came to our ears.
So we ran to the windows and opened the shutters.
We threw up the blinds to a sky full of udders.

"As lovely as angels," the family agreed,
And Elwood, so helpful, named each by its breed:
"Look, kiddies, a Holstein, a Brown Swiss, a Jersey,
And here comes a Hereford, an Angus, a Guernsey."

And so they did circle our satellite dish
To fulfill for dear Elwood an old Christmas wish—
That the Cows would return as they had in his youth,
And share with his family their goodness and truth.

Then over our intercom, we heard on the roofs
The tap-dancing clatter of the Santa Cows' hoofs.
"It's unreal," we exclaimed. "It's so strange. It's so weird."
Down the chimney the Santa Cows promptly appeared.

Now, light as a feather, they floated around
Over TV and pizza with nary a sound.
Then, after a while, they had floated enough
And touched down as gently as dandelion fluff.

Their eyes, like Liz Taylor's, were dewy and clear.
Their lips, like Liz Taylor's, so rosy and dear
As they smiled at us all from their warm inner glow.
And each of their tails was tied up with a bow.

They were good, they were warm, they were wise and, amen,
Just as Elwood had wished, they had found him again.
Then they sang us some carols, all limpid and light,
Like *Adeste Fideles* and *O Holy Night*.

Then the Holstein presented a beautiful tree
While, spellbound, we sat on Aunt Maxine's settee.
As we gazed at the ornaments, dazzling and rare,
A spirit of peace and goodwill filled the air.

There were bundles of *something* thrown over their backs.
We all tried to guess what might be in those sacks …
Maybe red-hots or gum balls or licorice whips,
Maybe squirt guns or skateboards or alien ships.

Then each of the Cows put a sack down before us.
Our "Oohs" and our "Aahs" then rang out in a chorus
As we opened the sacks. It was not as we'd thought!
It was baseballs and bats, gloves and caps that they brought.

Then we traced a great diamond outside in the snow,
And began with the Cows to hit, run, catch and throw.
So we played through the night, through each bright moonlit inning,
Till the sun showed its face. Christmas Day was beginning.

The artist's renderings were done in watercolor,
accompanied by pen and ink.
The text was set in Windsor Light by So Cal Graphics
of San Diego, California.
The title was handset in Windsor Comstock.
Designed by Judythe Sieck
Printed and bound by South China Printing Company, Ltd.,
Hong Kong